One Little Lot

The 1-2-3s of an Urban Garden

Diane C. Mullen · *Illustrated by* Oriol Vidal

Every day, the city is abuzz . . . as silent strangers hurry by without a glance.

ONE little lot sits abandoned
in the hustle and bustle.
Hungry honeybees buzz about,
searching for flowers to pollinate.
Until . . .

TWO helping hands push open
the rickety, rusted fence.
A visitor imagines what could be.
Passersby stop to talk.

Maybe, just maybe, they all say.

THREE long days are spent together—prodding, pulling, and preparing.

Old tires and broken bicycles are rolled away. Empty bottles are bagged up.

One little lot is ready for what's next.

FOUR planter boxes are installed in a straight, lovely line.

Like magic, they are built from weathered wood and shiny screws.

Hungry honeybees buzz around helping hands.

FIVE big bags of soil get emptied and edged into place.

One little lot is rich with black gold.
Worms wriggle around in this
composted dirt.

Be careful with the rakes!

SIX plentiful seed packets are opened and shared.
Neighbors sit side by side and gently tuck each
seed into its new home.

Grow, seeds, grow!

SEVEN showers pour over each sprouting seedling. Thousands of drops of water make the garden's journey possible.

Soon rangy roots begin to stretch

down,

down.

EIGHT rows line each planter box. Lush leaves reach up, up toward the shimmering sun.

Hungry honeybees buzz about,
pollinating many flowers, until . . .

NINE prized plants burst into a beautiful bounty!
Neighbors pick . . .

beans,

cucumbers,

bok choy,

carrots,

kale,

tomatoes,

kittley,

and peppers.

collard greens,

TEN newfound friends clean and chop and peel.
Together they cook and grill and sauté.

Hungry honeybees buzz above scrumptious smells, until . . .

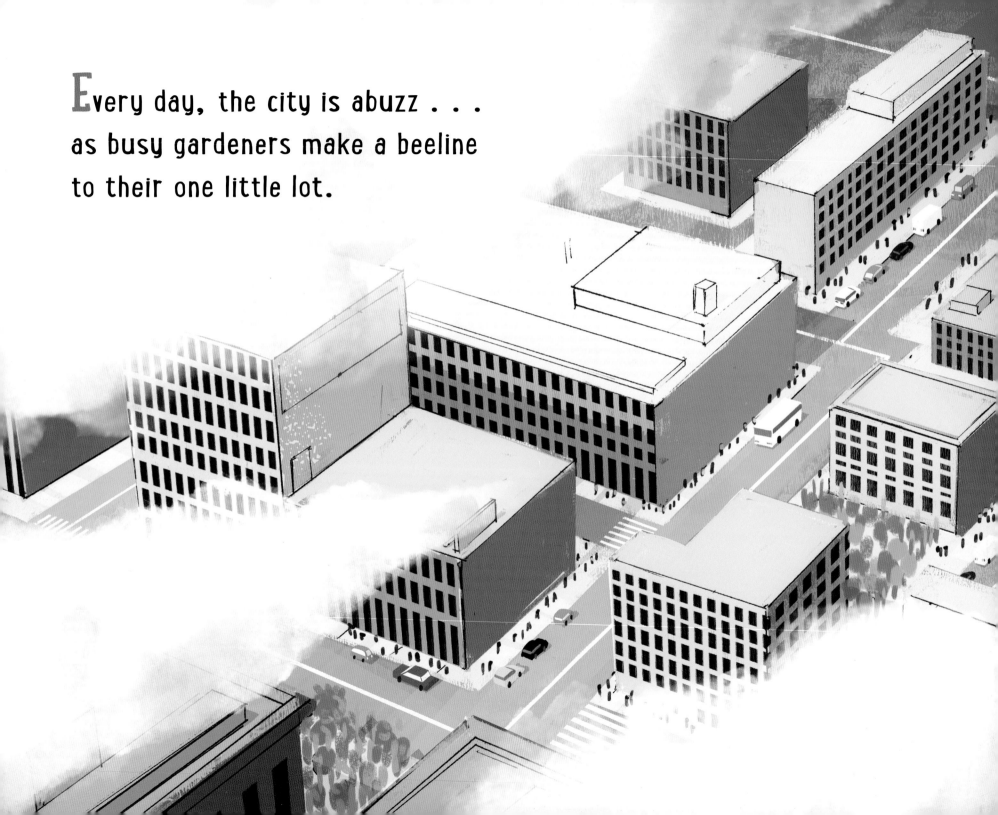

Every day, the city is abuzz . . .
as busy gardeners make a beeline
to their one little lot.

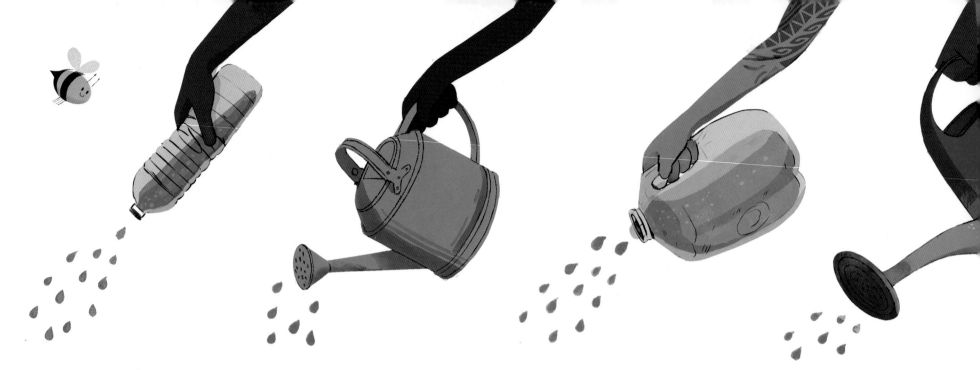

Author's Note

The inspiration for this book is my ten-by-ten foot plot of soil at the Soo Line Community Garden in the Whittier neighborhood of Minneapolis. It's not a big plot, and it's not a little plot. It's just right, and it's been mine for years. Our community garden is an oasis of growing greens surrounded by concrete, duplexes, apartment towers, and street art. In fact the mural in this book is inspired by a mural that was designed and painted specifically for the Whittier neighborhood by artists from Minneapolis College of Art and Design and area youth. I walk or bike past the beautiful faces on this vibrant piece of art daily.

Throughout the years, I've made dear friends in this community garden through something as simple as digging in soil and planting seeds of hope. Alongside my fellow gardeners—many of whom have come to Minneapolis from all over the world—I've grown vegetables, flowers, and lots of weeds. For me, our gardening is the perfect way to realize that we are all more alike than different, especially when our hard work is "full of delicious" and shared as friends.

All About Those Hungry Honeybees

The most important insects in this story and in my garden are honey bees. They're a welcome sight because without these hard-working little pollinators, we wouldn't be able to grow many foods we eat. Did you know that vegetables are flowering plants? When a bee lands on a plant's flower, it's

looking for pollen and nectar. Pollen provides protein and fats for the bee. Nectar is loaded with sugar and is a bee's source of energy.

Bees have tiny hairs on their bodies and legs. And when a bee lands on a flower, pollen sticks to those hairs. The bee then moves to another flower and transfers pollen from the previous flower to the next one. Each flower needs pollen from other flowers to make new seeds and turn to vegetables. Pollination is required for many garden vegetables, including collard greens, some okra, beans, squash, cucumbers, and more. Without bees and other pollinating insects, many plants would not get the pollen they need. No pollination means no food!

Ways to Make Your Little Lot Bee-Friendly:

1. Avoid pesticides because they're harmful to bees.
2. Use native plants that grow well in your area. Bees like plants they are familiar with!
3. Plant colorful flowers near your vegetables. Bees have strong color vision and are attracted to colorful blooms. Bees can transfer more pollen to your vegetable plants if they have more flowers to gather pollen and nectar from.
4. Plant your garden in a place that is sunny and where bees can find shelter from strong winds—like the sunny side of a fence, building, or wall!

Published by Charlesbridge
85 Main Street
Watertown, MA 02472
(617) 926-0329
www.charlesbridge.com

Library of Congress Cataloging-in-Publication Data
Names: Mullen, Diane C., author. | Vidal, Oriol, 1977- illustrator.
Title: One little lot: the 1-2-3s of an urban garden / Diane C. Mullen;
    illustrated by Oriol Vidal.
Description: Watertown, MA: Charlesbridge, [2020] | Summary: Count the
    ways two hands, three days cleaning up, four planter boxes, and many
    more steps show how city neighbors transform one little abandoned lot
    into a beautiful community garden.
Identifiers: LCCN 2018031381 (print) | LCCN 2018035421 (ebook) | ISBN
    9781632897527 (ebook) | ISBN 9781632897534 (ebook pdf) | ISBN
    9781580898898 (reinforced for library use)
Subjects: LCSH: Urban gardens—Juvenile fiction. | Urban gardening—
    Juvenile fiction. | Counting—Juvenile fiction. | Gardening—Community
    garden | CYAC: Urban gardens—Fiction. | Gardening—Fiction. | Counting. |
    LCGFT: Picture books.
Classification: LCC PZ7.1.M823 (ebook) | LCC PZ7.1.M823 On 2020 (print) |
DDC [E]—dc23
LC record available at https://lccn.loc.gov/2018031381

Printed in China
(hc) 10 9 8 7 6 5 4 3 2 1

Illustrations made with digital tools and mixed-media
Display type set in Lunchbox Slab by Kimmy Design
Text type set in Lunchbox by Kimmy Design
Color separations by Colourscan Print Co Pte Ltd, Singapore
Printed by 1010 Printing International Limited in Huizhou, Guangdong, China
Production supervision by Brian G. Walker
Designed by Diane M. Earley

For my daughter, Maggie, who has always
believed in the magic of *what could be.*
—D. C. M.

To my family—great fans of urban gardens!
—O. V.

A special thank-you to Minneapolis College of Art and Design alumna
and lead artist, Melodee Strong, and her team for creating the
Treehouse mural for the Whittier neighborhood. Designed with the
help of thirty-one youth and painted by 170 people, the mural
inspired the one illustrated in this book and is a true community feat!